P9-DCO-354

The
MYSTERIOUS MAKERS
of Shaker Street

SOUNDS
Like
TROUBLE

MAKER
SACK

STIRLING
LIBRARIES

K. DEC 2017

The Mysterious Makers of Shaker Street
is published by Stone Arch Books,
A Capstone Imprint
1710 Roe Crest Drive
North Mankato, Minnesota 56003
www.mycapstone.com

Copyright © 2018 Stone Arch Books

All rights reserved. No part of this publication may be
reproduced in whole or in part, or stored in a retrieval
system, or transmitted in any form or by any means,
electronic, mechanical, photocopying, recording, or
otherwise, without written permission of the publisher.

Cataloging-in-Publication Data is available on the
Library of Congress website.

ISBN: 978-1-4965-4676-0 (library binding)
ISBN: 978-1-4965-4680-7 (paperback)
ISBN: 978-1-4965-4684-5 (eBook PDF)

Summary: When Michael Wilson keeps hearing an
unusual sound at night, he calls on his friends Liv and
Leo to help him figure out what's causing it.

Design Elements: Shutterstock: Master3D, PremiumVector

Designer: Tracy McCabe

Printed in Canada.
10681R

The
MYSTERIOUS MAKERS
of Shaker Street

SOUNDS Like TROUBLE

by Stacia Deutsch
illustrated by Robin Boyden

STONE ARCH BOOKS
a capstone imprint

CHAPTER ONE

"Last night I heard the strangest noise."

Ten-year-old Michael Wilson was headed home. Walking along with him was his best friend, Leo Hammer, and his cousin, Liv Hernandez.

It was a warm day on Shaker Street. Michael tugged his baseball cap down to shade his dark brown eyes. He said, "It went *whirrrr whirl fzttt.*"

Leo ran a hand over his sandy brown hair. His bangs hung in his face. "Hmm . . . I don't know that one," he said. He readjusted the straps on his heavy backpack, then asked Michael, "Are you sure the *fzttt* was at the end and not in the beginning like *fzttt whirr whirl*?"

"Positive," Michael said. "Why?"

"Well if the *fztt* was at the beginning then I'd say you heard a 1997 Toyota station wagon with a loose fan belt," nine-year-old Leo explained. "But since the *fzztt* is at the end, I'm not sure what that could be." He shrugged. "It's a mystery."

"Mystery?" Liv, who was ten like Michael, was walking ahead of the boys. She spun around and pulled her headphones out of her ears. "I love a mystery!" Pressing a button on her phone, Liv turned off the sound.

"Sorry for ignoring you guys," she added. "I was listening to the last few minutes of *Alien Takeover.* I had to make sure the aliens didn't kidnap the poor old man."

Liv was the only one of them whose parents had gotten her a phone. Leo's dad and Michael's parents agreed that they didn't need one yet. It was a huge bummer.

Michael rolled his eyes at Liv and snorted. "You know that podcast is a hoax, right? There's no scientific proof that extraterrestrial life is real."

"And there's no proof that it's not real," Liv said. She peered over her red vintage glasses frames. "What do you think, Leo?" Liv pinned him with her deep brown stare.

"I —" Leo hesitated. "If there really are aliens, I'd prefer it if they'd stay on their own planet."

"Ah, so you *do* believe in aliens!" Liv exclaimed, grinning. "Leo's the smartest kid at school. Best grades. Best scores. HA!" She faced Michael and put her hands on her hips. "That's all the proof you need," she said. "Aliens exist."

"You're ridiculous," Michael argued. "That's not proof. Besides, Leo's a chicken. If there was a chance that aliens might land on Shaker Street, he'd be at home hiding under the table."

"True," Leo agreed. He tucked his hands into his armpits and clucked. "Bawk, bawk."

Liv insisted, "I'll prove it to you both that the podcast —"

BANG! A firecracker burst over Michael's house. The sparkles glittered in the late afternoon sky.

"Forget the aliens! We gotta go! Now!" Michael shouted at his friends.

They were still near Liv's house at the bottom of Shaker Street. Michael's house was pretty far away, at the dead end at the top of the hill.

The Wilson home was one of the biggest on the block. And it was the tallest.

The old Victorian looked like a skinny purple painted gingerbread house with green icing trim. Above the third floor was a tower room — a turret, Michael's mom called it. There were lots of windows that overlooked the other historic homes of Shaker Street.

Michael saw a flash of light in one of those big windows. Then, as the fireworks faded, a familiar voice boomed through a loudspeaker in the front yard.

"You have five minutes!"

The voice belonged to Michael's grandfather, Henry Wilson Senior.

Michael regretted the day he'd built those small speakers for his grandfather. He'd used two cool-looking tin cigar boxes to hold the wiring. They were supposed to make Grandpa's stereo louder, so his old ears could hear his favorite music. But Grandpa immediately rewired them.

Grandpa thought it was funny that he'd turned the speakers into an announcement system that echoed throughout the entire neighborhood. No one else thought it was funny at all. Especially not Michael. It was embarrassing — for Michael *and* his friends.

"Ticktock," Grandpa called out. His eighty-year-old voice cracked.

"Ugh," Leo groaned, looking up the tall hill. "I hate it when he does this." He tightened his backpack straps for the run. "Someone should call Sheriff Kawasaki."

"She wouldn't do anything," Liv said. "The speakers are annoying, but everyone on Shaker Street loves Grandpa Henry." Henry Senior was Michael's dad's, Henry Junior's, dad. Liv and Michael's moms were sisters, so Liv wasn't related to Henry Senior. Still, she and everyone else called him Grandpa.

Just then the old man called out, "Time's a wastin'."

"Ugh," Leo complained again as they took off running up the hill. "Maybe you could invent some kind of escalator," Leo said to Michael as his breath became heavier. "Or a zip line."

"A zip line that goes up?" Michael asked. He looked at Leo. His friend was slowing down to walk. "That would be against the laws of gravity."

"Some laws need to be broken," Leo said. His face was turning red and sweaty.

They were partway up the hill, nearly at the mustard yellow, weathered house where Leo and his dad rented the second floor.

Nervous that Leo might duck out for a snack and a nap, Michael took his friend's arm. He tugged Leo the rest of the way up the hill, while Liv pushed from behind.

"Come on. We're almost there," Liv said, encouraging Leo to keep going.

"Ticktock," Grandpa's voice cackled through the loudspeaker. "Three minutes and twelve seconds to go. Or else!"

CHAPTER TWO

Michael, Liv, and Leo dashed through the purple house's side gate. They went straight to their Maker Shack Clubhouse.

The clubhouse used to be Grandpa Henry's toolshed. When Michael was old enough, Grandpa gave it to him as a place to hang out and build things. Now Grandpa thought it was fun to lock Michael and his friends out of it with traps.

Michael pulled on the door. To no one's surprise, it was locked.

"What's the situation?" Liv asked, pushing up her glasses. She hovered over Michael's shoulder.

Michael surveyed the locks on the shed door. There was usually only one lock. Michael had the key. Today there were five different ones. They had twisting combination dials instead of keyholes. He twisted the first dial randomly.

"Ticktock," Michael's grandfather called out of an upstairs window. "You have one minute, fifty-eight seconds."

"That's not long enough!" Liv sighed. "The old guy never gives up, does he?"

"We've got this," Michael assured her. He took a closer look.

Michael continued. "So, the first thing I notice is that these combination locks have letters instead of numbers." He turned to Leo. "Can you find any information about this type of lock?"

"You can use my phone," Liv said, rubbing it in that she had one and they didn't.

"Maker Shack Rules," Michael reminded them both.

"Fun killer," Liv muttered, even though she knew the rules. One of them was no phones at the clubhouse. Michael and Leo had made that one up. Since she was the only one with a phone, Liv was outvoted.

But computers were allowed.

"It's okay." Leo swung his backpack to the ground. "I like a big screen." He took out his laptop. "Booting up. Hang on."

While Leo searched the Internet, Liv said, "This whole thing reminds me of the alien podcast! A man called in —" She stopped talking to think for a moment about the story.

Michael looked to Leo with a desperate face. "Hurry."

"You need to rig me some faster Internet!" Leo told Michael.

Liv patiently continued her story. "The caller in the podcast said that aliens had captured him and locked him into their spaceship. They were about to blast off, taking him away from Earth forever, when he realized the code to the lock was made of letters —"

"A cipher!" Leo jumped up and gave Liv a high five. "Michael, it's a code. Each lock takes one letter. They're all connected."

"So we need to figure out a five-letter word to get inside," Liv concluded.

Michael thought about his grandfather and the locks. He realized something important.

While he thought Liv's favorite podcast was silly nonsense, Grandpa loved that same show. "Liv, is there any chance the voice of the caller was familiar?"

"Hmm." Liv bit her bottom lip thoughtfully. "He did have a husky voice that cracked like Grandpa Henry's." She glanced up at Michael's grandfather. He waved at her from the attic window.

"We know it was you!" Michael shouted.

His laugher resonated from the tower.

"Was he really abducted by aliens?" Liv asked Michael.

"Of course not," Michael answered. "He knew you'd be listening to the show. You know Grandpa. It was all part of this set up." With only a minute left, Michael talked fast. "What was the code the aliens used in the story?"

"ALIEN," Liv said.

"Of course," Michael said with a glance at his grandfather's window. It looked like he was dancing in the attic.

"Are you sure he wasn't really abducted?" Liv asked. "They don't let you on the air if your story isn't true."

"It's not true," Michael assured her. "Think about it. Why would aliens want an old guy like him? He's not a very good specimen. They'd be better off with someone like Leo!" Michael laughed as Leo gasped in horror.

With quick fingers, Michael moved each of the lock dials to a letter.

ALIEN

"There." Michael stepped back to see what would happen.

The locks were still locked.

Michael looked at Liv. "Was there anything else interesting in the story?"

"The man, I mean your grandfather, said he had to press a button at the bottom of the last lock. The button opened all the locks. Then, he ran away from the alien's wicked grasp," Liv said.

Sure enough there was a tiny little hole at the bottom of the fifth lock. Michael tried to poke in it with his finger. When that didn't work, he looked for a tool.

"Forty-two seconds!" Grandpa Henry's voice boomed through the loudspeakers.

Michael looked again at the release button. It was bigger than a paper clip. But smaller than a pen cap. He had a idea.

"Leo, give me your shoe." Leo's tennis shoes were always untied.

Leo took off his shoe and handed it to Michael. Michael pressed the small button at the bottom of the last lock with the hard part at the end of the shoelace — the part that's called an aglet. "Come on, ALIEN," he begged.

Click, click, click, click, click.

The locks swung open.

"Wahoo!" Liv shouted.

"We did it!" Michael pushed open the door to the Maker Shack. Before he went inside, he waved up at his grandfather.

"You had two seconds to spare!" the old man shouted. He smiled and gave the kids a thumbs-up.

"What would have happened if we didn't solve the code?" Liv asked Michael as they entered the dusty clubhouse.

Michael shrugged. "I don't know." He closed the door behind them and said proudly, "We've always solved it."

"Can I have my shoe back?" Leo asked. He held out his hand.

As he sat down to tie up his shoe, Leo noticed a new photo hanging on the wall. "I see you've been decorating," he said.

The picture showed Michael with his mom and dad, Grandpa Henry, Liv, and Leo. They were gathered around a table with a large chocolate cake in the middle. Michael had been adopted as a baby. The picture was taken at his adoption anniversary celebration the week before.

Grandpa had used an antique camera. He attached a self-timer made from a wire hanger and string. That's how he snapped the shot. No fancy "telephone gadgets" were allowed when Grandpa Henry was around.

"Grandpa must have hung it up here," Michael said. He picked up the picture for a better look. There was something lumpy pressed into the back of the frame. Turning it over in his hand, he found a note.

It said:

Someday I'll outsmart you little whippersnappers!

CHAPTER THREE

"Tell us more about the funny noise you heard," Leo said to Michael. "Was it spooky?"

Every corner of the Maker Shack was crammed with Michael's tools and discoveries. There was a chair at a desk. He made it out of a board on top of two brick stacks. Leo took his usual seat at the desk and set up his computer. Michael plopped down on a stool by the workbench. The bench was made from an old door set on top of piled fruit crates.

In the corner was Liv's bright blue beanbag chair. Michael had found it in a dumpster and cleaned it up for her. Liv loved that chair. She'd decorated the entire corner around it. There were leafy plants and a basket for all her magazines.

Liv plopped down in her beanbag with a whoosh. From her basket she picked up a copy of her favorite newsletter. It was called *Suspicious Surprises*. "This month is all about how to chase away ghosts," she said happily. She began skimming the articles while Michael described the sound he'd heard.

"It wasn't a normal sound," he told his friends. "But it wasn't spooky."

Leo hooked up his laptop to a microphone that Michael had found at a yard sale. "Make the noise again. I can search the web for what it might be," Leo said.

Leo typed commands into his laptop, which was another of Michael's Maker Space projects. The laptop had been Leo's dad's boss's and was headed for the trash. Michael had rescued it and given it new life.

"*Whirrrr whirl fzttt,*" Michael said into the microphone, repeating the sound a few times. Leo made a recording. Then Leo scanned an online database.

Liv set down the newsletter. "You say you only hear this mysterious noise at night?" she asked Michael.

"Yeah. Every night for the past week." He hadn't told his friends at first because he thought it was just an animal or something like that. But as the noisy nights went on, he changed his mind. Michael decided it was definitely something more unusual than a stray cat or a raccoon.

Michael said, "Last night, I woke up Mom and Dad so they could listen. But they didn't think it was weird. And Grandpa can't hear anything after he takes out his hearing aids."

"So what do you want to do?" Liv asked. Her eyes followed Michael as he paced around the shed.

"Phase One is see if Leo can identify the noise," Michael said. He looked over Leo's laptop screen. The words *NO MATCH* were blinking rapidly in bright red letters as the computer continued to search. "Phase Two is to go out at midnight tonight to investigate."

"Yay for Phase Two!" Liv cheered.

Leo moaned. "Come on, baby." He patted his laptop with a loving hand. "Give me what you've got." *NO MATCH* continued to light up the screen.

"We're going to need supplies," Michael told Liv.

"What are we making?" she asked. She looked over the Maker Shack bins of wires and electrodes and metal cases and wheels. All the bins were marked in pen with labels declaring what was inside.

"A sound amplifier," Michael said. He pulled down boxes from the shelves and piled them next to Leo at the workstation. "Human ears are limited. To hear what's going on, we need to make the noise louder and clearer."

Liv raised her eyes. "I think there's an app for that . . . Come on, Michael. Let's use my phone. Just this once."

In response, Michael clicked his tongue and pointed over Leo's head.

There, posted in the center of the longest wall, were the rules for Mysterious Makers of Shaker Street.

The large piece of cardboard had come from a refrigerator box flap. It read:

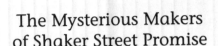

The Mysterious Makers
of Shaker Street Promise

1) We turn old things into new things.

2) We don't use new things if we can use old things.

Leo had scribbled at the bottom:
Computers are okay.

Liv had added:
Phones are okay if zombies attack. Call me!

The last line read:
This contract is legally binding.

The last part was also Leo's addition.
His dad was a lawyer, and he wanted the
document to sound official, even if it was
made out of cardboard.

Liv, Michael, and Leo had all signed the
agreement in permanent pen.

"Oh well." Liv sighed. "How's the
computer search, Leo?"

"I got nothin'." Leo's computer search
had come to an end. There was no matching
sound.

With a frown, he reported, "I was hoping
it was the call of a rare bird. Maybe the
happy yip of a fuzzy bunny rabbit." Leo
knew what was coming next. "I guess we're
going with Phase Two?" he asked.

"Yes! Phase Two!" Liv jumped around
clapping her hands.

Michael began opening bin lids, looking under box tops, and piling supplies on the counter. "This is going to take a while," he said, pinching his lips together. "We need to stay up late, so . . ." He raised an eyebrow. "I'm sure my parents will agree — you're both invited to a sleepover."

"A *creepover* is more like it," Leo said with a grunt. "We're spending the night listening to some spooky noise."

"You don't have to stay," Liv said. Her cheeks were flushed with excitement. "You could go home."

"I know," Leo said. But as scared as he might be of what they might find, Leo was first and foremost a loyal friend. Liv and Michael both knew he'd never leave. Especially when there was a mystery to solve.

CHAPTER FOUR

Leo slept over all the time. His dad was fine with it as long as Leo called before bed to say good night.

Liv's parents were divorced. Her mom lived on Shaker Street. Her dad lived a few blocks away. Since Liv and Michael were cousins, they often stayed at each other's houses.

"Since I'm staying here, Mom's going to have a movie marathon with CoCo," Liv said when she hung up the phone. CoCo was five and liked shows about musical animals. "There's no such thing as a singing bear," Liv said, rolling her eyes. "That's so unrealistic!"

Michael and Leo laughed. Then they went into the big house for dinner.

A few hours later, the three of them returned to the clubhouse. Michael had most of what he needed for the amplifier laid out on the worktable.

"Do you want me to look up how to make one?" Leo asked.

"Nah," Michael said. "I'm sure we'll figure it out." He already had a few ideas of where to start.

He picked up an old tape recorder. It was a small silver box with a speaker on the front. A mini tape cassette went into a slot. A thick gray button played the tape, which was a rectangle about the size of two thumbs side-by-side.

"Wow," Leo said, looking at the recorder. "Where'd you get that?" They always tried to find parts for the things they made. Dumpsters and garage sales were the best places for Maker Shack treasures.

"This was my mom's," Michael said. "When she started selling houses, she used it to record her customers talking about what they wanted. Then she'd help them find the perfect place."

"She's the best house seller on Shaker Street," Leo said. "But I'm glad she's using her phone now." He smiled.

"I know," Michael said happily. "If she was still using a tape recorder, we wouldn't have one!"

Michael set the recorder on the workbench. "I found it in a drawer of junk," he said.

He got a pair of earphones, the kind with the long wire. The recorder had a speaker, but the sound would be clearer — and more private — through the earphones.

Liv was going through a box of small microphones that could be plugged into the tape recorder.

"If we can hear sounds from around the neighborhood," she held up the smallest microphone in the bin, "do you think we could amplify sounds from outer space too?" She raised the microphone to her mouth and said, "Anyone out there?"

"You can't hear something that doesn't exist," Michael said.

He snatched the microphone and was about to plug it into the tape recorder. But stopped. He looked for some wire. It would be better to put the microphone on a long wire. That way the recorder could be near the computer, and the microphone could pick up sounds that were outside and further away.

He measured out some extra wire. Attached it. Then plugged in the microphone. There were two input slots. He put earphones in the second hole.

"It's ready." Michael stuck a small cassette tape into the recorder. He held the whole thing in the palm of his hand. "Let's try this out."

"I'll go into the yard," Liv suggested. "I'll start pretty far away. See if you can hear me. I'll move around to test it."

"When we find you, I'll run your voice through the computer. If we use a GPS, maybe we can track where you are," Leo suggested. His fingers were already typing commands into the laptop. "It's like hide-and-seek for Liv."

"If you can't find me, shout out 'Olly, Olly Oxen Free!'" Liv laughed. She left the clubhouse and disappeared through the gate toward the front of the house.

Michael set the tape recorder on the workbench. He stretched out the microphone wire, pointing the microphone toward the place he last saw Liv. He stopped the motor on the recorder, so there'd be no interference. Then Michael put the earbud in his ear.

"Can you hear her?" Leo asked. "Once you get sound, we'll put the earbud next to the computer. I can record the sound and get an ID."

Michael closed his eyes. "I hear . . . breathing."

"Oh, sorry," Leo said, slamming a hand over his mouth. With hand motions, he asked Michael, *Can you hear anything now?*

Michael shook his head.

Leo let out his breath. "Whew," he said. "I thought I might explode."

"Impossible," Michael assured him, then listened some more. He shook his head. "It's not working."

"The microphone isn't strong enough to reach Liv," Leo said. "She has to come in closer."

"Not yet," Michael said. His eyes flitted around the room, searching his supplies. "We just need a way to get the sound to come through louder."

"An antenna?" Leo suggested. "What else makes things louder?" He cupped his ear with his hand and joked, "Eh? I can't hear you."

"That's it! Good thinking, Leo!" Michael exclaimed.

"You're welcome," Leo said even though he didn't know what he'd done.

Michael ran to get a box of poster board left over from school projects. He took out a piece of fluorescent pink board, recycled from Liv's science fair project, and rolled it into a cone. Then he put the microphone in the cone.

"It's like how your cupped hand focuses the sound," he explained.

Sticking the cone and microphone outside the window, he could clearly hear Liv now.

"Hang on," Leo said, typing on the keyboard. "Pass the earphone. I'll pinpoint her location in a second."

"Forget it," Michael said with a laugh. "I know where she is."

He turned up the amplifier's volume so they both could hear from one bud.

"Were you scared? Did they try to shoot at you with their laser eyes?" Liv was rattling on and on.

Michael looked to Leo and said with a chuckle, "She's on the front porch with Grandpa."

"I'm sure he'll keep her busy with stories until midnight," Leo said, pulling two remote controllers out of his backpack. "Want to play video games?"

Michael checked the clock. It was three hours until midnight. They had tons of time. "Sure," he said, taking the red controller. "What do you want to play?"

Leo winked and said, "Let's shoot space aliens."

CHAPTER FIVE

At exactly midnight, Michael and Leo
tiptoed out of Michael's room. Liv was in the
guest room at the end of the hall. She snuck
out and met them at the bottom of the stairs.

"This way." Michael led his friends out the
back door to the Maker Shack Clubhouse.
"Whew," he said, noting that his grandfather
hadn't messed with the locks again . . . yet.

They entered the clubhouse and Liv picked
up the sound amplifier.

"I really wish we could hear aliens," she said. She held the cone, with the microphone in it, toward the sky and shouted, "Anyone out there?"

"*Shhh . . .*" Michael put a finger over his lips. "We don't want to alert whoever's making the sound."

"Or wake up Michael's parents," Leo said as the computer booted up.

Michael took the listening device. He put the earbud next to the laptop and turned up the volume.

"There!" Michael said, looking at Leo's computer screen. A little green light was bouncing all around. That meant the strange sound was coming through.

"Can you figure out where it's coming from?" he asked Leo.

Leo began to use a GPS to locate the source. A minute later he said, "It's too far away." He leaned back in his chair and said, "Since we can't find out what it is, I think we should go back to bed . . . where it's safe."

"*Whirrrr whirl fzttt.*" Liv imitated the noise. They were all hearing it clearly now. "Sorry, Leo. I think it's coming from somewhere on Shaker Street. Let's walk slowly down the hill to find out exactly which house."

"No thanks," Leo insisted. "We should stay right here. When there's trouble, it's always the little, slow guy who gets caught."

"True," Liv told him, winking at Michael. "But we'll rescue you. Don't worry."

"Ugh." Leo groaned.

"We're gonna need a few things." Michael began pulling bins off the shelves.

He grabbed a backpack from a low shelf. "This is our new Maker Shack Maker Sack," he explained. He set the old, dirty, dark blue pack on the worktable. "I found it in a trash can behind school. I don't get why someone tossed it out."

"Uh, because there's a hole in the bottom," Liv said. She stuck her hand all the way through and wiggled her fingers at Michael.

Michael replied, "It's still good." He handed her a roll of heavy-duty silver duct tape.

Liv smiled. "I'll fix it." She taped up the bottom of the bag while Michael ran around the shed and Leo packed up his laptop. When the backpack was ready, Liv wrote "Maker Sack" on the front in strips of the silver sticky tape.

Michael then stuffed the Maker Sack with things he thought they might need: a suction cup, a wire hanger, alligator clips (which are wire with clips on the end), some extra long pieces of wire, a penny, a few nails, and three small LED bulbs.

"We need one more thing," Michael said as they snuck out of the clubhouse. He took one of Grandpa's blasting speakers from the front porch and stuck it in the Maker Sack.

"I'll put everything back tomorrow," Michael told his friends as he slipped the backpack over his shoulders.

"Maybe not Grandpa Henry's speaker," Leo suggested with a grin. "No one would mind if it disappeared."

"He'll just make a new one," Michael assured Leo. "Even louder."

Michael helped Leo slip a strange contraption around his neck. It was made of bungee cords and an old man's leather briefcase. The briefcase hung like a portable table for Leo to put his computer on, so he could walk and type at the same time. Using a Wi-Fi booster from the clubhouse, Leo could keep his laptop and the GPS system running all the way down Shaker Street.

Liv had the amplifier. She listened to the sound, then tried to guess which way to go.

Leo had the GPS. Running the *whirring* sound through his computer, Leo could figure out which way it was coming from. "This direction," he said, leading them.

Streetlights lit their path. They passed Michael's neighbor to the left. Liv pointed the amplifier's cone toward the house on the right.

They still weren't close to the noise that Michael heard. It was still too far away. Slowly, they made their way down the street.

"Oof!" Liv stopped so suddenly that Leo bumped her in the back. "Oof," he said again, stumbling into the yard of a two-story, plain-looking, beige house with a FOR SALE sign in the yard.

Liv reached out to steady Leo with one hand. "The sound's definitely coming from this one," she reported.

Michael took the amplifier and made sure it was directed at the house. Then he checked that the earphone was sending the sounds through Leo's laptop.

The three of them listened quietly to the *whirrrr whirl fzttt* sound while Leo scanned the noise.

"It's definitely here," Leo said. There was a shiver in his voice. "But the sound isn't coming from inside the house." He clicked a few buttons on his laptop. "I've looked at the GPS coordinates. And checked the math three times. The equations check out. That sound is coming from under the house."

CHAPTER SIX

"My mom's actually selling this house," Michael said as they walked slowly around toward the backyard. "No one has lived here for months."

"Weird," Liv remarked, wrinkling her eyebrows. "So what do you think is in there, Michael? Ghosts? Zombies? Huge, genetically modified rats?"

"A person." Michael said flatly, picking up a piece of paper near the fence.

He held up the burger wrapper and added, "Just one hungry human being."

Liv shook her head, then her eyes widened. "Maybe it's a vampire! If it's a vampire, we shouldn't go in. We don't have the right supplies."

"A vampire who likes cheeseburgers?" Michael asked. "I don't think so."

"Maybe he ordered the meat rare?" Liv said, acting insulted that Michael would even ask.

"Vampires? Rare meat? I gotta go," Leo said. He started to disconnect himself from the laptop carrying case. "I hear my dad calling."

Michael chuckled. "He's asleep." To prove it, he pointed the sound amplifier toward Leo's house. "I can hear him snoring."

Leo's shoulders slumped. "We cannot break into this house. Nope. No way," he said. "Sheriff Kawasaki would be here in a flash. I can't have an arrest on my college record."

"You're only nine years old," Michael said, raising an eyebrow.

"I know," Leo said. "I like to think ahead."

"I'll admit this is scary, but I'm sure it's a person in there. A normal person." Michael told Leo.

"We don't have to break in," Liv told Leo. She leaned over the side fence and pointed. "The back door's open."

"That seems bad —" Leo began. But before he finished his sentence, Liv and Michael were through the gate and into the open door.

From inside the house, Liv leaned her head through a small open window. Soft white curtains billowed around her face. She pushed them back and whispered, "Bring the computer, Leo. Hurry."

Leo groaned. "First thing tomorrow, I'm getting new friends," he said. Tightening his computer carrier straps, he headed into the abandoned house.

"We don't need the amplifier anymore," Michael said. He stopped in the small kitchen to put it in his Maker Sack. The glow of a streetlight gave them enough light to see.

"Look at that," he told the others. There was a hole in the floor behind a narrow staircase. The stairs went up. The hole went down.

"Oh, boy," Leo shivered and sighed.

The *whirrrr whirl fzttt* sound had stopped. "Maybe whoever, or whatever, is making that noise went home for the night?" he said.

"We're checking it out," Liv told him. "Leave the laptop here. We'll get it on the way back."

Reluctantly, Leo took off his computer carrier and set it on the kitchen counter next to a roll of papers, rubber banded like a tube. He pointed at the papers.

"I wonder what those are," Liv said with a shrug. She started to unroll them when the *whirrrr whirl fzttt* sound started up again. It came from underneath them and echoed through the kitchen.

Liv put down the papers, and they hurried to examine the hole in the floor. There was a rope ladder swinging down from where they stood. It was impossible to see the bottom.

Michael stepped onto the ladder to go down first. He ran a finger over his lips, reminding Leo and Liv to be quiet. When he reached the bottom, Michael shook the ladder as a signal for the next person to start.

Liv came down.

When it was Leo's turn, he grumbled softly the whole way.

At the bottom, it was completely dark. Michael reached out and gently touched Leo on the shoulder. Liv's hand brushed Michael's, so he knew they were all together.

The three of them snuck, silent as mice, through the tunnel. Michael was in the lead. He wished he'd thought to bring a flashlight in his Maker Sack.

He'd brought LED bulbs, but that just seemed silly now. What was he thinking? Bulbs with no battery?

Michael decided that when they got home he'd put a permanent flashlight in the Maker Sack — just in case.

For now, it was too late. They couldn't see, but he knew they were getting closer to the source of the noise. The *whirrrr whirl fzttt* was getting louder.

They went forward, very slowly. The tunnel was much longer than Michael expected. They walked for a while.

In the distance, Michael could make out the end of the tunnel. Slivers of light shone through cracks in the wall to reveal a shape looming at the end.

It looked like a long tube with sharp blades on the front. Almost like a drill with a shovel. Michael had never seen anything like that. It was so strange looking. He wanted a closer look.

Edging forward, Michael was leading his friends toward the odd machine when suddenly, he saw movement in the shadows.

Michael gasped. It was a man.

The man turned toward Michael.

Michael stopped quickly and ducked down. They needed to stay out of sight. He put up a hand as a signal to tell Liv and Leo to stop too. But the space was too dark. Liv hit Michael's hand and bounced back. Then, Leo smacked into Liv and yelped, "Oof!"

The man's voice rang out. "Who's there?" The *whirrrr whirl fzttt* stopped, and suddenly a flashlight shined their way. "Who's there?" the voice shouted again.

In a hard whisper, the man said, "Ghosts be gone," which Michael thought was very odd.

"Be gone!" the man shouted in a louder voice.

A clanging noise began. It sounded like a spoon hitting a metal pot.

"Run!" Michael whispered to his friends. He pushed at Liv in the darkness. "To the ladder!"

No one needed to tell Leo. Michael could hear him climbing up. He must have taken off the instant the man shouted at them.

All three Makers got up the rope ladder in seconds, but the man from the tunnel was right behind them.

"In here!" Liv motioned toward a large pantry in the kitchen. There was plenty of room to hide inside. She closed the door behind Leo.

"Wait." Leo ducked back out.

He grabbed his laptop from the counter and took the roll of papers. "In case we need to hit someone with it," he said, swinging the tube like a bat.

Again, Liv closed the door behind them. They didn't dare to breathe as the man entered the kitchen.

His heavy footsteps clicked against the tile. He grumbled something that sounded like, "Haunted," then disappeared out of the room. The footsteps faded.

Liv cracked open the pantry door. Moonlight from the window lit the space. She made sure the man was gone, then she looked around their hiding place.

"For an empty house," Liv said in a whisper, "there sure is a lot of food in the pantry."

"I wonder what he's up to," Michael said to the others. They were keeping their voices soft, just in case the man heard them. Michael searched through the bags and found chips, dry pasta, and a basket of lemons. "Looks like he's been living here," he said.

"I bet he goes away in the day and comes back at night," Leo told Michael. "He can't risk that your mom might come in to show people the house."

"Who's gonna buy this house now? There's a hole in the floor," Liv reminded them.

Micheal considered the hole for a moment. "He must cover it," he concluded. "It would be easy to hide the hole with a wood board and some carpet."

Liv took the tube of papers from Leo. She removed the rubber band and spread the papers out on the kitchen counter, where the moonlight was bright enough to read by.

After studying the drawings for a long moment, Liv gasped.

"I know what he's doing," she said, voice rising. "He's making a tunnel from this house all the way to this building at the end of the street." With a long finger, she traced the path between the buildings. "Look! The tunnel ends in the Shaker Street Bank's vault." She tapped the plans. "He's going to rob the bank!"

CHAPTER SEVEN

"We have to stop him," Michael said, pacing the kitchen. The *whirrrr whirl fzttt* sound had begun again below them, and now Michael knew what it meant.

The thief was back at work in the tunnel. He was running the machine. And Michael knew exactly what that contraption did.

The *whirrrr* was the motor of a huge digging drill. Those were the sharp blades he'd seen.

The *whirl* was a scoop removing dirt and setting it aside. That was the shovel he'd noticed.

The *fzttt* was the machine resetting over and over again. It would dig a little, then dump out the dirt. Reset and do it again.

He'd seen slivers of light. That meant the tunnel was almost at the bank.

The drill was so loud, Michael and his friends could walk and talk normally. The man wouldn't be able to hear them.

"How are *we* going to stop the crook?" Leo asked. "We gotta call the sheriff."

"The man might run away," Liv said. "We're here now." She put her hand on Leo's arm. "We can do this on our own."

Leo released a heavy breath, but he didn't argue.

"Fine," he said, giving in. "What's the plan? We can't see in the tunnel. How are we going to stop someone we can't see?"

Michael began dumping things out of his Maker Sack onto the countertop. "I've got this," he muttered. "Liv, grab a couple lemons from the pantry."

She gave a sideways confused look to Leo but grabbed two lemons.

"Three would be better," Michael said. "But let's try this." He stuck pennies in each lemon. Then he put nails in the opposite side of the fruit.

"I know what he's doing," Leo told Liv, quietly so as not to interrupt Michael's focus or to attract the man under the house. "Batteries are made of two metals in an acid solution."

"The nail is one metal," Liv said, watching Michael connect alligator clips to the nails. "The penny is copper, so that's a second metal."

Michael connected a nail from one lemon to a penny in the other. Then he connected the other penny to the little LED bulb he'd put in the Maker Sack. And from the second lemon, he connected a nail to the bulb.

When the circuit was complete, the bulb began to glow!

It was faint, but the lemon light was going to be just enough. They could see where they were going.

"Cool," Liv said, admiring the "flashlight" that Michael had made.

He grabbed four more lemons and made two more lights — one for each of them.

Then Michael said, "Let's go catch a bad guy."

Michael put the Maker Sack on his back.

Leo booted his laptop up for a second, typed into the keyboard, then shut it all back down.

"If he escapes," Leo said, "I don't want him taking my laptop with him." He set the computer on a shelf in the pantry and blew it a kiss. "See you soon," he said and shut the door.

They made their way back down the ladder. Liv stopped them at the bottom. "Uh, Michael. The lights are great, but how are we going to catch this guy?"

In the glow of the lemon lights, Michael thought they all looked spooky. They looked like ghosts — which of course, didn't actually exist.

Michael had a practical idea. "We'll get him to chase us into the street."

"Then what?" Leo asked.

Michael had already considered that. "Then Leo goes to the neighbor to call the sheriff," he said.

"Already done," Leo said with a grin. "I emailed her a minute ago. I told her to come to the middle of Shaker Street as soon as possible. I said that she'd find a crook there. Luckily, she checks her email regularly!"

"I guess we better get this thief outside then," Michael said, glad that Leo and Liv were with him. He needed his friends. "The problem is that the tunnel is a dead end on his side," Michael explained. "We have to make him run toward us because he has to go up the ladder."

Liv raised her light to her face, making her look extra spooky. "That's too dangerous. Leo might get caught."

The way she said it, Michael knew she was teasing, but it was a real possibility. "We need the thief to leave the house without catching us," Michael said.

"How are we going to do that?" Leo asked.

"I know. We'll scare him out. He's afraid of ghosts," Liv told them.

"What are you talking about?" Michael said a bit too loud. He lowered his voice, and simply grunted, "Huh?"

Liv explained, "Remember that article I read earlier in the *Suspicious Surprises* newsletter? The one about scaring ghosts away? The article suggested banging on a pan with a wooden spoon."

She smiled and continued, "I think the thief read that same article. That's what that sound was after he yelled at us. He thought we were ghosts."

"He even said, 'Haunted,'" Leo said with a smile. His teeth looked yellow in the faintly glowing light.

"We just have to convince him the house — and the tunnel — are really, truly haunted," Liv said with confidence. "He'll be so scared that he'll run into the street and straight into Sheriff Kawasaki's handcuffs."

"So now we have to figure out how to scare him . . . ," Leo said. He looked to Michael. "What else do you have in that sack?"

Michael grinned, putting the bag on the floor of the tunnel and opening the zipper. "I've got exactly what we need."

"If I take apart the earbuds and attach the wires to Grandpa's speaker . . . ," Michael muttered to himself as he worked in the glow of all three lemon lights, "I can plug the speaker into the tape recorder. Instead of a sound amplifier, it'll blast sound like a PA system."

Suddenly the *whirrrr whirl fzttt* sound stopped.

"Oh, no! I think he's taking a break," Liv whispered to Michael. "Are you done? We gotta get out of here!"

"I'm done." Michael pushed past Leo to reach for the ladder. "Hurry. Let's go upstairs. Just in case he's going to the kitchen for a snack. We can hide somewhere until he's back in the tunnel."

They all agreed.

Very quietly, Michael stepped rung to rung until he reached the top. Liv followed.

"Oof!" That was the sound of Leo falling off the ladder. "I missed a rung!" He shouted as he scampered up again.

The voice from the tunnel started to boom, "Who's there? Is anyone there?"

A few moments later, Leo shouted, "Help! He's got me!"

CHAPTER EIGHT

"The rest of you, get back down here now," the thief threatened. "Or else."

"No one ever says what 'or else' means," Liv told Michael with a groan. "Why can't it be 'Or else we'll have cookies?'"

"Help!" Leo shouted again. "*Heeeellllp!*"

Liv turned to Michael. "Quick, can you make it sound like there's a ghost in the tunnel?"

"On it." Michael pressed record on the tape recorder so that the microphone would blast sound through the speaker. "*Oooh, oooh . . .* ," he started.

"Is that seriously what you think a ghost sounds like?" Liv took the tape recorder and microphone from Michael's hands. She left him holding the speaker.

Then Liv started screaming in a high-pitched wail. "You have disturbed my burial grounds!" Her voice blasted through the speaker.

Michael leaned over the tunnel to let the speaker hang down. "It'll echo," he told Liv. "Keep going."

"Let the boy go . . . ," she cried out. "Or else!" There was no response from down in the tunnel.

Liv put down the microphone. She asked Michael, "What are we going to do?"

"We gotta save Leo," Michael said. He was starting to panic. "This is all my fault!"

Liv bit her lip, then said, "I have an idea. Can you get those fruit lights going again?"

"Of course," Michael confirmed. He checked the connections and handed Liv a lemon light.

Liv looked around the house. "I need the curtains," she said, dashing over to the back door. When Liv came back a second later, she was wearing a curtain over her head. She stuck a fruit light underneath it so the curtain glowed.

"Wow," Michael said, feeling goose bumps pop out all over his arms. "If I believed in ghosts, I'd swear you were one."

"I'm going into the tunnel," she said, mustering up her courage. "You can be my voice."

"I can't," Michael told her. "I'm a terrible ghost." To prove it, he said, "Oooh . . ." one more time. He grabbed his backpack and pulled out several very long pieces of wire. "I'm going to rig the microphone so you can take it with you," Michael told her.

With fast fingers, he twisted wires together and attached them to the microphone. The cord was now long enough that Liv could carry it wherever she went. He'd stay back, slowly unwind the wire for Liv, and hold the speaker so the sound would echo through the whole tunnel.

Michael helped Liv carry the curtains and the lemon light down the ladder. When they reached the bottom, he said, "Go save Leo."

She nodded, then began to pretend she was a ghost. "Now you have angered me," she said in her scary voice. "I am coming to get you. Watch out . . ."

Michael could see the glow from Liv's curtain costume as she disappeared into the darkness. Then he heard the banging. The spoon was slamming against the pot. He knew the thief was scared.

"Away, evil spirit," the man shouted.

"Liv, get back here," Michael whispered into the shadows. "I think this is too dangerous."

She didn't answer. He didn't think she could hear him over the sound of the speaker.

"You cannot escape my wrath!" Liv shouted into the microphone. Her voice crackled.

"I knew this house was haunted!"
The thief was banging his pot wildly and
screaming, "*Aaaaaaauuuuuuugh!*"

The thief knocked Liv over on his way to
the ladder. Michael ducked to the side, just
in time. The man rushed past him, climbed
the ladder, and ran screaming out the front
door of the house.

The police sirens were loud. Michael knew the sheriff had gotten Leo's email. She was there in time. The crook was captured.

Liv appeared back through the tunnel. "Good ghost," Michael told her. He peered into the darkness. "Where's Leo?"

She took off her costume and they went in search of their friend. They found him at the end of the tunnel. He was sitting against the farthest wall, behind the digging equipment.

"Leo?" Michael was worried the thief had hurt his friend. "You okay?"

"I-I-I," Leo stuttered. "I-I-I . . ."

Liv sat down on the floor next to him. "What happened?" she asked.

"I saw a ghost!" Leo jumped up. "It was wearing white and speaking in this spooky voice. And its face glowed!"

Leo was shaking as he pointed down the tunnel toward the exit. "It was right there!" he said.

Liv started to laugh. Michael laughed too.

"What?!" Leo insisted. "Don't make fun of me. I know what I saw, and it was terrifying."

"It was me," Liv told him with a smile. "I'm the ghost."

"No way!" Leo said. He refused to believe his friends.

"Let the boy go . . . or else," Liv said in her ghostly voice. "I used a lemon light under the house curtains." She held up the little light that was now illuminating the tunnel.

Leo studied Liv's face for a long moment, then nodded. "And her voice went through your speaker?" he asked Michael.

"Yep," Michael admitted.

Michael was sure that Leo would be mad that he'd gotten caught in their trap to scare the thief, but instead he started to giggle. "There's no such thing as ghosts," Leo said, feeling better.

"Right," Michael said.

"At least not in this house," Liv corrected them.

They all followed Liv's lemon light to the ladder and up into the kitchen.

Sheriff Kawasaki was standing by the pantry. She held Leo's laptop in one hand and the thief's plans for the tunnel in the other.

The sheriff was young with shoulder-length black hair and fierce eyes that could scare a crook.

Her family had moved to Shaker Street from Japan when she was a baby. She grew up on this street and now was sworn to protect it.

"Does this belong to you?" she asked, holding out the laptop to Leo.

"Uh-huh." He took it, nodding sheepishly.

Michael wondered what she'd say to them. Were they in trouble?

"We've taken Mr. Slater into custody," she told the kids. "He was a tunnel engineer who decided to start robbing banks. For years, he's been tunneling under houses all over the world. Now, thanks to all of you, he's going to jail."

"Awesome!" Liv cheered, raising her hand to high-five the boys.

The sheriff stopped her.

"Not so fast, young lady." The sheriff had her intense eyes pinned on Liv's face. "You shouldn't be here." She looked from Michael to Leo and back to Liv. "It's late. You're trespassing and breaking and entering. Plus you stole curtains and lemons that didn't belong to you." At that, Liv set her lemon light on the counter.

"Give me one reason why I shouldn't arrest you," the sheriff said, looking from Michael to Liv and back to Leo. "If you can convince me, I'll let you go."

CHAPTER NINE

Liv plopped down into the beanbag chair at the Maker Space Clubhouse. "I can't believe she let us go!"

Michael took a seat at the worktable, while Leo plugged in his computer.

"She didn't let us go, exactly," Leo said. "Your mom, my dad, Michael's parents, and even Grandpa Henry are in house having a 'conference.'" He made air quotes with his fingers.

"Conference schmonference." Liv leaned her head back into the beanbag. "We aren't in jail," she said. "And I'm telling you, the sheriff was happy for our help."

"She didn't seem happy though," Michael said. He imitated the way she sideways stared at them with one dark eye. "In fact, I think it was the opposite."

"Nah." Liv yawned. "She was happy. Without us, Mr. Slater would have robbed the Shaker Street Bank and gotten away with it." She stretched her arms above her head and yawned again. "Catching crooks is hard work."

"Yes it is," Sheriff Kawasaki said as she entered the clubhouse. "And that's why catching crooks should be left to the sheriff." She pointed at herself.

Liv went to stand beside the boys as all the adults came into the clubhouse. It was crowded in there with so many people.

Michael gave a small wave to his parents, who shook their heads as if to say, "What were you thinking?!"

Liv's mom had a flat expression. It was as if she expected to discover Liv sneaking around an old house at night.

Leo's dad looked tired. He stood closest to the sheriff, with his eyes on Leo. Leo shrugged. His dad shrugged back. In some ways, it looked to Michael as if Mr. Hammer was proud of Leo for overcoming his fears to help catch a thief.

The only one smiling was Grandpa Henry. His grin stretched ear to ear. "Now that's my boy!" he cheered.

All the parents instantly glared at him. "What?" he asked innocently. "These kids are heroes." Michael would have laughed if Sheriff Kawasaki wasn't giving him that evil side-eye.

"Your parents and I have agreed," the sheriff began. "Going after a thief on your own wasn't smart. But," she went on, "it turned out to be helpful."

"Heroes, I tell ya," Grandpa cut in, raising a victory fist.

The sheriff shot him a warning look.

He stepped back.

"So," she turned her hand toward all the adults, "we have agreed — no one is grounded. No one is in trouble."

Michael looked at his friends. That was not what he expected.

"And no one ever does anything else like this ever again."

That was what he expected.

Liv was the first to agree. "Got it," she said.

"Understood." Leo hugged his dad.

"No more sneaking around at night," Michael promised, going to stand between his parents.

The sun was rising when Leo, Liv, and Michael followed the group back into the big house. They were going to sleep for a few hours, then make something new in the clubhouse.

"I told you the sheriff was glad we helped," Liv said as they stood together in the hallway, before going to separate rooms. "Did you see her wink?"

"What wink?" Michael and Leo said at the same time.

"The one she gave us just before she left," Liv said. "The one that meant we should help her out solving crimes whenever we want."

"What are you talking about?" Leo asked Liv. He wrinkled his eyebrows and stared at her.

"I didn't see anything," Michael said. "In fact, I think we all promised *not* to snoop around Shaker Street anymore."

"You weren't listening." Liv shook her head. "You need to hear words that aren't said. Sheriff Kawasaki just hired the Makers of Shaker Street to be on the lookout for anything suspicious. It's our job."

"Are you sure?" Michael asked. There was no way . . .

"Positive," Liv said, opening the door to the guest room and giving a big yawn. "We start tomorrow."

YOU CAN BE A MYSTERIOUS MAKER TOO:

LEO'S LOUD AMPLIFIER

Things to find:

- Earbuds with wire attached
- Microphone
- Small tape recorder
- Cassette tape for the recorder
- Tag board

TRY THIS!
If you add foil to the inside of the tag board tube, the reflective surface should increase the sound even further.

Directions:

1. Put the tape in the recorder.
2. Plug the earbuds into the correct jack.
3. Plug the microphone into the other jack.
4. Press the record button and the pause buttons together.
5. Create a cone from the tag board. Tape it together.
6. Tape the microphone into the cone.
7. Turn up the volume. You should be able to hear the sounds coming from the microphone through the earbuds.

MICHAEL'S TAPE RECORDER MEGAPHONE

(Continued from steps 1–7)

8. Exchange the earbuds with a portable speaker.
9. Press record and pause together.
10. Use the microphone. The sound should come out the speaker.
11. Make your own ghostly growls.

LIV'S LEMON LIGHT

Things to find:

- 2 Lemons
- 2 Pennies (must be before 1982 so there is enough copper content) or two copper wires
- 2 Galvanized nails
- 3 Test lead alligator clips (a clip with a wire attached to either end)
- LED bulb

Directions

1. Put a nail and a penny into the skin of each lemon. Make sure there is space between the nail and the penny.
2. Attach a test lead alligator clip from the penny on one lemon to the nail on the other.
3. Attach a clip from one nail to the LED.
4. Attach a clip from one penny to the other LED.
5. If your light isn't glowing, try adding more lemons to the chain.

ABOUT THE AUTHOR

Stacia Deutsch is the author of more than two hundred children's books, including the eight-book, award-winning, chapter book series *Blast to the Past*. Her résumé also includes *Nancy Drew and the Clue Crew*, *The Boxcar Children*, and *Mean Ghouls*. Stacia has also written junior movie tie-in novels for summer blockbuster films, including *Batman*, *The Dark Knight* and *The New York Times* best sellers *Cloudy with a Chance of Meatballs Jr.* and *The Smurfs*. She earned her MFA from Western State where she currently teaches fiction writing.

ABOUT THE ILLUSTRATOR

Robin Boyden works as an illustrator, writer, and designer and is based in Bristol, England. He has first-class BA honors in illustration from the University of Falmouth and an MA in Art and Design from the University of Hertfordshire. He has worked with a number of clients in the editorial and publishing sectors including Bloomsbury Publishing, *The Phoenix* comic, BBC, *The Guardian*, *The Times*, Oxford University Press, and Usborne Publishing.

GLOSSARY

abduct (ab-DUKT)—kidnap someone

amplifier (AM-pluh-fye-ur)—a piece of equipment that makes a sound louder

amplify (AM-pli-fye)—to make something louder or stronger

contraption (kuhn-TRAP-shuhn)—a strange or odd device or machine

cipher (SYE-fer)—a message in code

database (DAY-tuh-bayss)—a collection of information that is organized and stored in a computer

electrodes (i-LEK-trodes)—points through which an electric current can flow into or out of a device or substance

extraterrestrial (ek-struh-tuh-RESS-tree-uhl)—coming from outer space

interference (in-tur-FIHR-uhnss)—something that interrupts sound or vision so that it does not work properly

specimen (SPESS-uh-muhn)—a sample used to stand for a whole group

TALK WITH YOUR FELLOW MAKERS!

1. The Mysterious Makers of Shaker Street have several club rules, including no phones. How would the book have been different if they would have used Liv's phone?

2. The Mysterious Makers think of themselves as inventors. What are some characteristics of good inventors? Do the Makers have these characteristics?

3. At the end of the book, Liv is convinced the sheriff wants the Makers' help patrolling the neighborhood. Do you agree with her? Why or why not?

GRAB YOUR MAKER NOTEBOOK!

1. Compare and contrast yourself with one of the Mysterious Makers. How are you alike? How are you different?

2. Pick a scene in which you disagreed with how a character handled a situation. Rewrite it in the way you think it should have happened.

3. Think about the scene where the thief is scared by Liv. Try rewriting it from the thief's perspective. What is he thinking? How is he feeling?

THE FUN DOESN'T STOP HERE:

Discover more at www.capstonekids.com

- Videos & Contests
- Games & Puzzles
- Friends & Favorites
- Authors & Illustrators

Find cool websites and more books like this one at www.facthound.com. Just type in the Book ID: 9781496546760 and you're ready to go!

READ MORE MAKERS ADVENTURES!